Growing Readers

New Hanover County Public Library

Purchased with
New Hanover County Partnership for Children
and Smart Start Funds

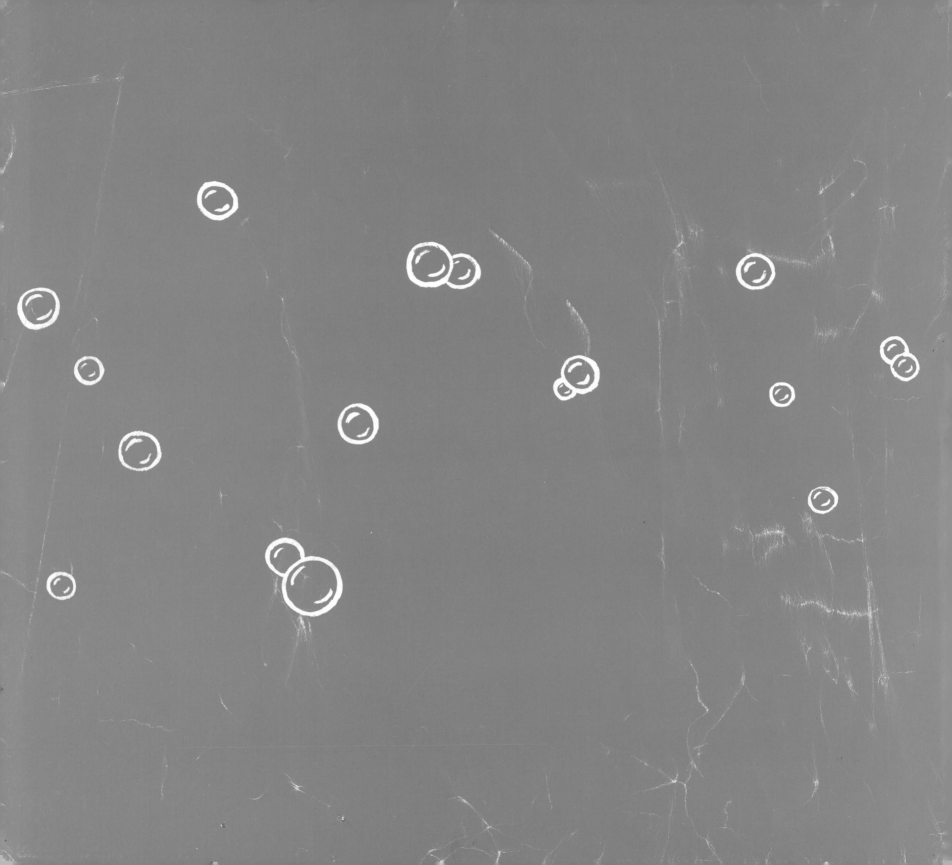

Rub-a-Dub Sub

Linda Ashman   Illustrated by **Jeff Mack**

Harcourt, Inc.   *San Diego   New York   London*

To Jean and her water bugs—
Rich, Justin, Bradley, and Brennan
—L. A.

For my mom and dad
—J. M.

Library of Congress Cataloging-in-Publication Data
Ashman, Linda.
Rub-a-dub sub/Linda Ashman; illustrated by Jeff Mack.
p.   cm.
Summary: A young boy meets many friendly sea animals as he travels underwater
in his bright orange submarine.
[1. Submarines (Ships)—Fiction.   2. Marine animals—Fiction.
3. Stories in rhyme.]   I. Mack, Jeff, ill.   II. Title.
PZ8.3.A775Ru   2003
[E]—dc21   2002004794
ISBN 0-15-202658-4

First edition
H G F E D C B A

Manufactured in China

The illustrations in this book were painted in acrylics on Arches Aquarelle
180 lb. watercolor paper.
The display type was set in Stone Informal Bold Italic.
The text type was set in Plantin Bold.
Color separations by Bright Arts Ltd., Hong Kong
Manufactured by South China Printing Company, Ltd., China
This book was printed on totally chlorine-free Enso Stora Matte paper.
Production supervision by Sandra Grebenar and Wendi Taylor
Designed by Suzanne Fridley

Special thanks to Jack for your love, encouragement, and editorial advice—
and a really excellent title!
—L. A.

Sinking in my

submarine,

my sub

glub glub

marine.

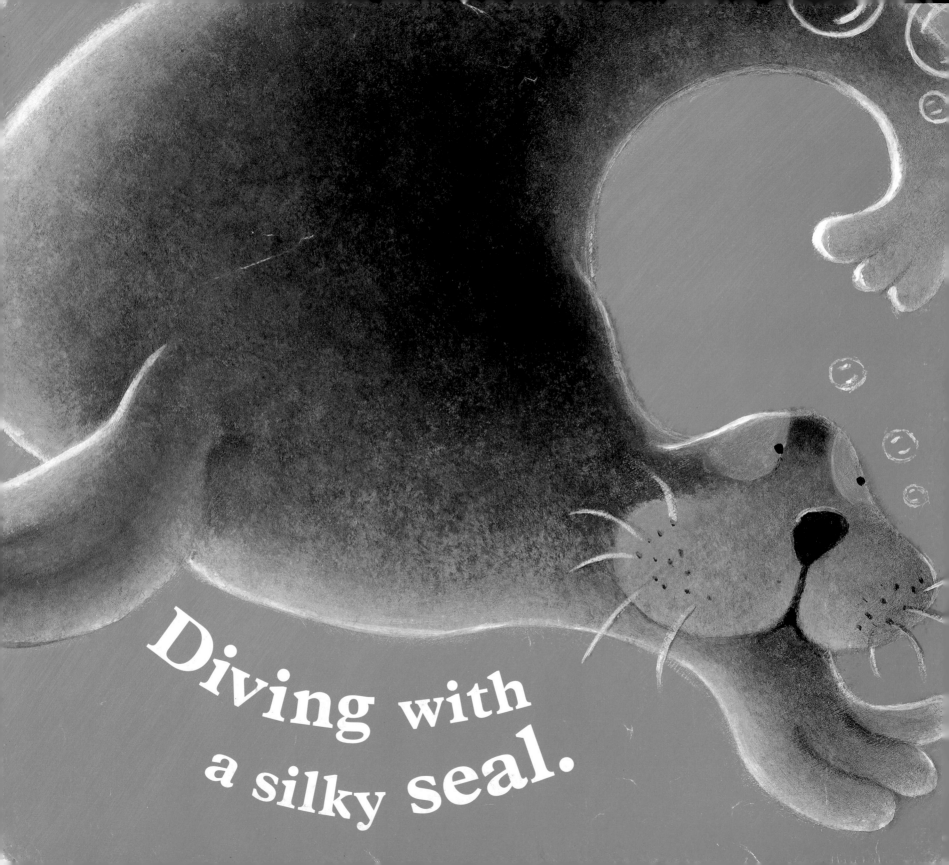

Diving with
a silky seal.

Darting by a dancing eel.

Peering through
a kelpy haze

at rainbow fish
and manta rays.

Waving to a whiskered shrimp.

Floating by a blowfish-blimp.

In the darkness,
something pink—

sub is sprayed
with murky ink!

Hiding from the horseshoe **crabs.**

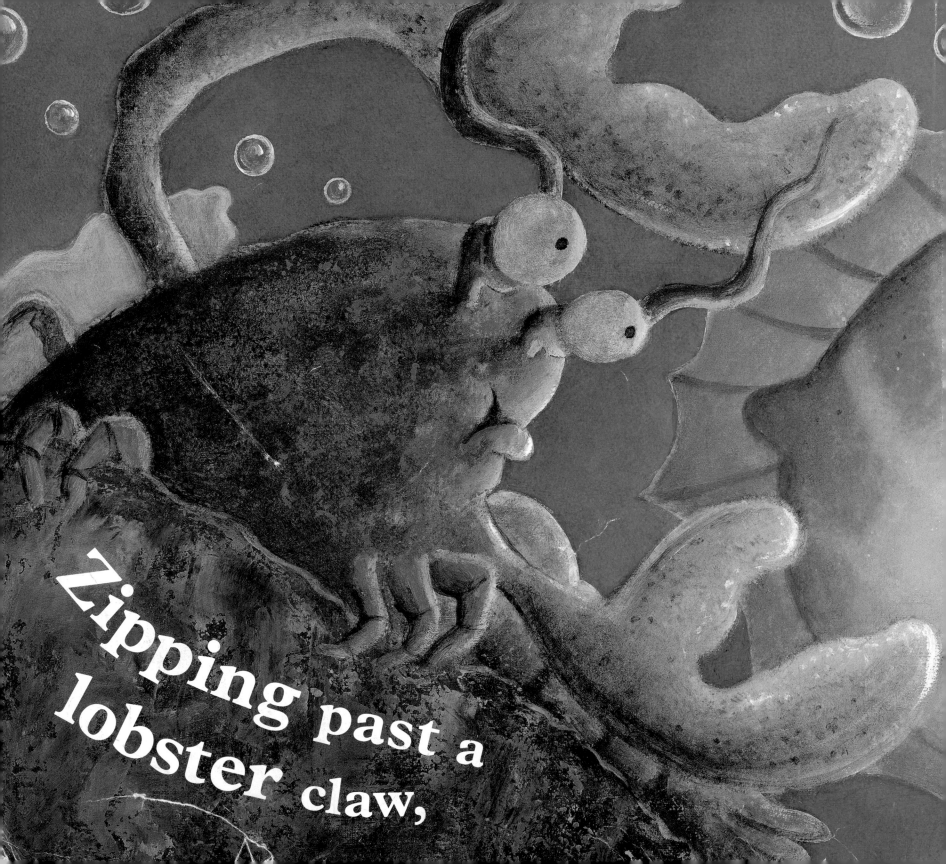

Zipping past a lobster claw,

miss a marlin's pointy jaw.

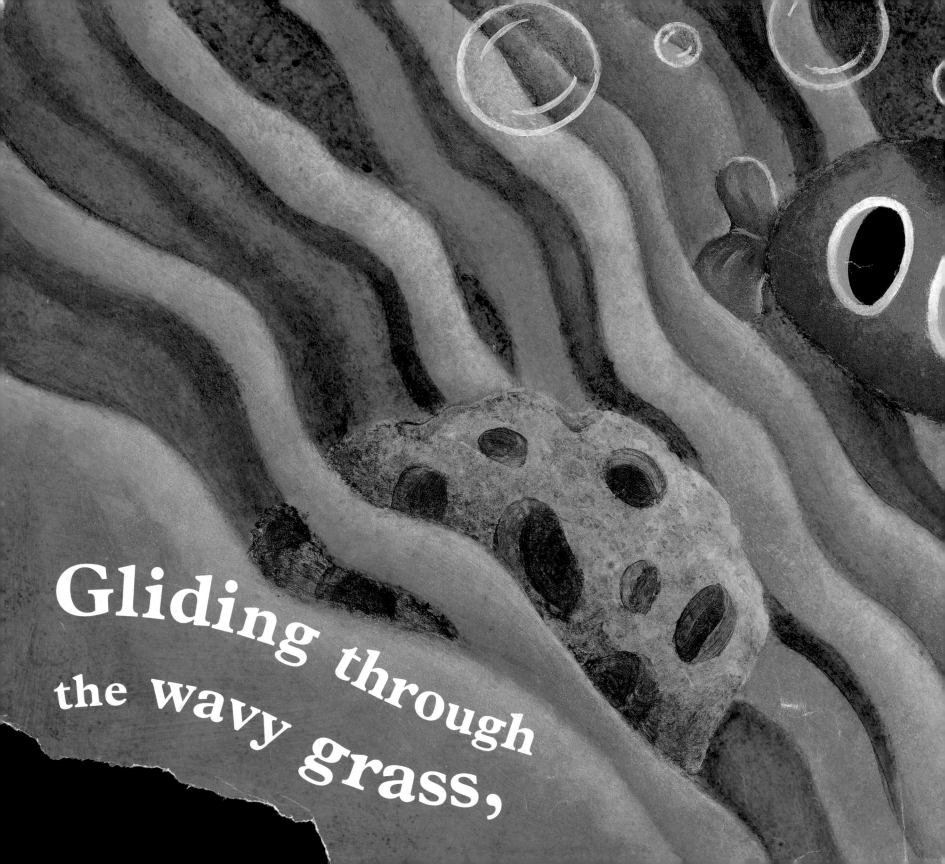

Gliding through the wavy grass,

glimpse a busy
cleaner wrasse.

Dropping deeper
in the dark,

meet a sleek
and speedy. . .

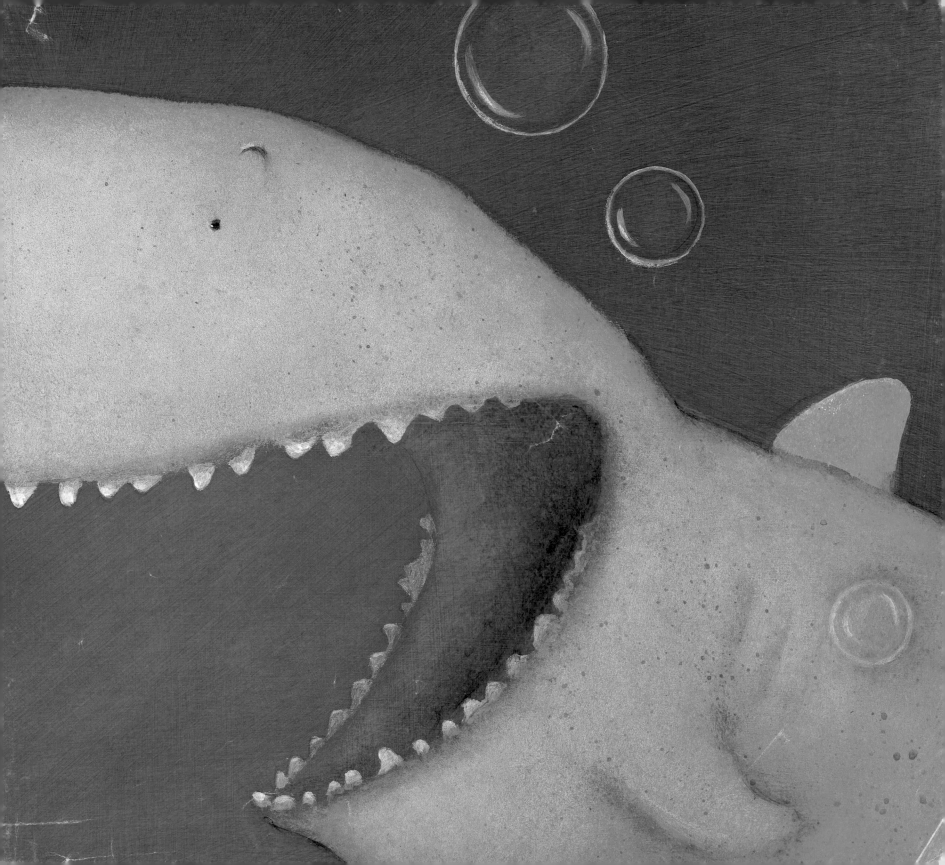

Brush the blimp!

Bump the shrimp!

Race the rays!

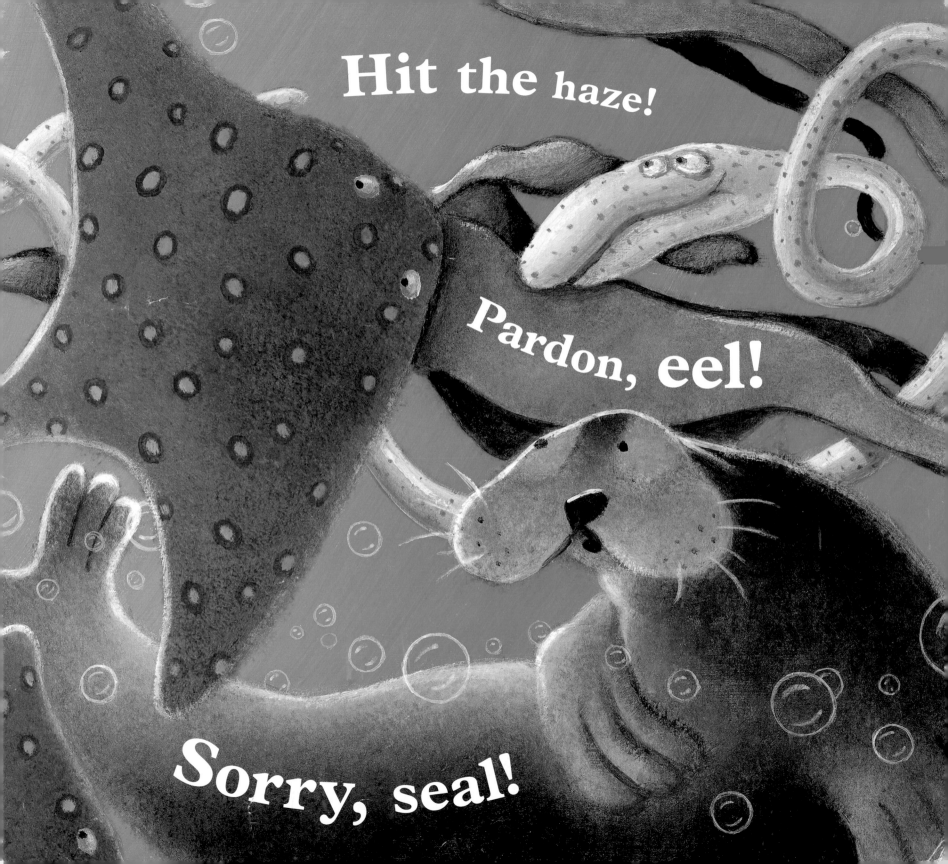

Rising
quickly
in my **sub,**

to the
safety
of my...

tub.

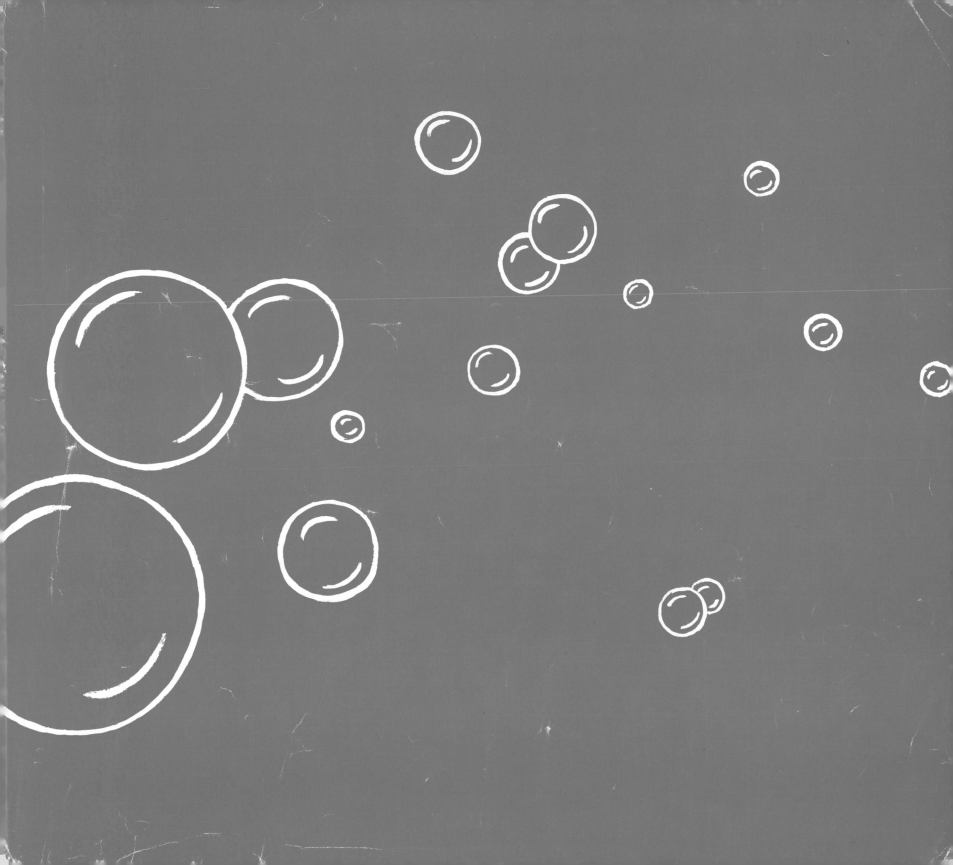

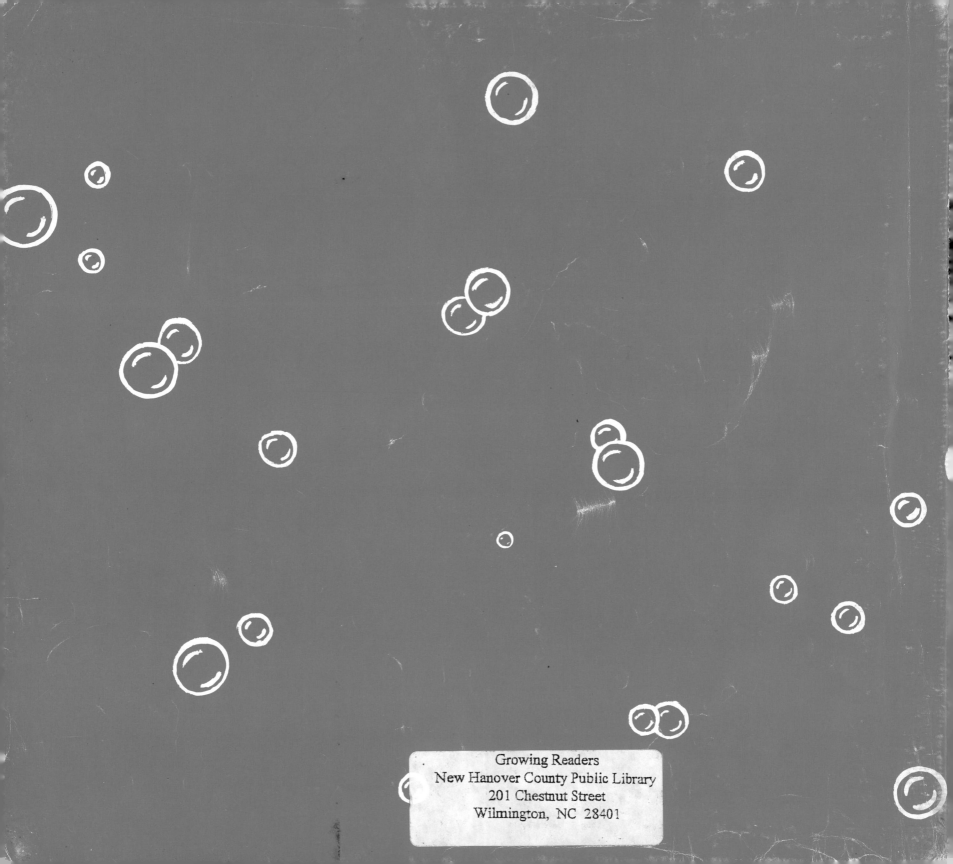